WHAT IF......

........You Could Go Back in Time

"Time travel... will never be impossible forever."

—Toba Beta, *Betelgeuse Incident*

GLENDA JENSEN

Copyright © 2023 by Glenda Jensen

ISBN: 978-1-77883-020-4 (Paperback)

All rights reserved. No part of this publication may be reproduced, distributed, or transmitted in any form or by any means, including photocopying, recording, or other electronic or mechanical methods, without the prior written permission of the publisher, except in the case brief quotations embodied in critical reviews and other noncommercial uses permitted by copyright law.

The views expressed in this book are solely those of the author and do not necessarily reflect the views of the publisher, and the publisher hereby disclaims any responsibility for them.

BOOKSIDE Press

BookSide Press
877-741-8091
www.booksidepress.com
orders@booksidepress.com

Shout Outs

There are so many people whom I would like to dedicate this first novel to; however, there are a few that really stand out:

First of all, I dedicate this novel to my Lord God who gave me the talent to put my imagination into words.

I would like to dedicate this novel to my high school sophomore English teacher, Mrs. Walthal. She was the first to get me started to write. I was 16 years old at the time.

To all the students that walked through my classroom door who listened to my ideas, inspired me to write, and helped me to encourage them to write.

For my grandparents who all told me stories about family as I was growing up. In fact, I have written some short stories just about those told tales.

To my family who gave me material to write and encouragement to continue.

Contents

Chapter One: **Present Day** 3
Chapter Two: **Back in Time** 5
Chapter Three: **A Hopeful Day** 10
Chapter Four: **The Witch** 13
Chapter Five: **The First Victim** 15
Chapter Six: **The Second Victim** 18
Chapter Seven: **The Request** 21
Chapter Eight: **The Evidence** 26
Chapter Nine: **The Tenth Victim** 28
Chapter Ten: **The Ritual** 31
Chapter Eleven: **The Save** 34
Chapter Twelve: **The Return** 38
Chapter Thirteen: **Jason and Family** 41
Chapter Fourteen: **The Final Piece of the Puzzle** 45
Chapter Fifteen: **Wendy's Story** 48
Chapter Sixteen: **Another Visit to the Past** 51
Epilogue 57

WHAT IF..........

(Introduction)

Time. The clock ticks; an alarm sound. We are surrounded and ruled by time. Time tells us when to go to school or work; time tells us when to come home. The past is past, and the future is yet to come. But the question at hand is: can time be manipulated or changed?

What if the invention of a time machine or the discovery of a time portal were possible? **What if** you could return to that time when you cheated on a test and decided not to? **What if** you could return to that time when you could actually act on that serious crush you had in high school? **What if** you could return to a time when you could save a person's life? **What if** there was a way for you to return? Would you? What would you change? Why?

We have read stories similar to The Time Machine by H. G. Wells and read stories like A Sound of Thunder. In The Time Machine, the main character travels towards the future and discovers what happens to mankind. If it was possible, would you walk through the door and embark on a different kind of adventure? In the story, A Sound of Thunder written by Ray Bradbury, strict orders were given NOT to do anything that would alter the future. In Bradbury's story, a hunting party is allowed to travel back in time to the dinosaur era in order to hunt extinct animals. However, one member steps off the path and accidentally steps on a butterfly. When they get back, their present had been changed catastrophically. There were rules, and the men kept going back to make things right. But **what if** there were no restrictions and you could return to a time which you wanted to change? Would you?

This story tells about a sixteen-year-old girl named Sharon who had those exact thoughts. This is a story about the repercussions of those thoughts. This is the story of a detective who uncovered the truth.

For four years, sixteen year old Sharon agonized over an event that was to haunt her for the rest of her life. For four years, she battled depression, moodiness, antisocialism, plummeting grades, and yes, dabbled in the world of drugs in order to forget. But almost overnight, she discovered a solution that would put an end to all these problems and a willingness to live again. Her discovery would give her a chance to make things right and for her family to be whole again. What she did not know and should have known is that there IS a reason for everything. Her only thought was to bring harmony back into her family. Yet, the harmony she hoped for would soon turn into evil.

Chapter One

PRESENT DAY

Detective John Morgan was a 10-year veteran in the Dallas Police Department. In his ten years as a detective on the force, he has never experienced a serial murder quite like the case he was just handed. His previous experience was out in Anaheim, California, a suburb of Los Angeles. Throughout his 25 years as a police officer, he had arrested murderers, thieves, molesters, prostitutes, and drug kings. Yes, he thought he had seen it all, but this was different and more gruesome. When Morgan learned of a position as detective in Dallas, Texas, he did not hesitate to pack up and move his family. He thought that he was getting away from all the horror and maliciousness of a large city. They lived in the city of Richardson, a suburb of Dallas, just to be sure. He thought Richardson would be the perfect place to raise his three now teenage children, but now he was having second thoughts.

The balding forty-five-year-old man, who looked like he ate one too many donuts and hadn't been to the gym in years, sat at his desk drumming his fingers as he was looking at the folder which held evidence for 10 similar murders. Morgan's smile was one that could light up any room but not today. He just sat looking at these cases perplexed and disgusted all at the same time. When he came to work this morning, his attire was crisp. His pants were pressed, and he even sported a new tie, a gift from his wife. But now he looked like he slept in those same clothes. These cases gave him goose bumps, something no other case had done before. They were all women, the victims, that is; they all had been dumped in a wooded area just south of Dallas along with no available forensic evidence. But there was something similar about these women. They all resembled each other. All had light brown hair with blue eyes. They were all young, too. But it was the way they were killed that made his stomach churn. He began to think of his wife and his three boys. He was concerned for their safety but especially the kinds of influences that his boys would be exposed to. He looked at their picture on his desk and said a silent prayer over them.

Morgan then went back to the folder that he was looking at. Suddenly, a figure walked up to him and seemed to loom over his very being. At first, Morgan was startled but then realized it was his partner, Shelley Anderson. Shelley was a beautiful 32-year-old brunette with blue eyes and a curvaceous figure, someone that anyone in the precinct would give a month's pay just to have a date. But Shelley was all work, and it helped to have a father who was Assistant District Attorney named James Anderson. Shelley was moved up to the detective department about five years earlier when she passed her test. She and Morgan had been partners ever since.

Morgan handed the file to his partner. "Tell me what you think," he said. "We may need to call the BAU (Behavior Analysis Unit of the FBI) for this one." As she was thumbing through the file, she asked him, "why?" "You don't think you can handle this one, Mr. 100% homicide cases solved?" He chuckled and said, "I guess you got me there. If we dig deep, we can find this guy and put an end to these senseless murders." What Morgan did not know at this time was that this case was going to prove to be his most challenging one. They both got a cup of coffee and began to pour over the case files looking for any kind of thread of evidence and leads.

Chapter Two

BACK IN TIME

Sixteen-year-old Sharon Leanne Foster, Shar to her friends, lay on her back on her bed in her bedroom. With her dyed black hair spraying across her pillows, she could not help but stare at the ceiling wondering what her future will hold. Her parents were always arguing, and she found herself crying all the time. Sharon just could not get a grip on what happened four years ago. Even with the gothic posters and black lights within her sight, the visions of that day still haunt her day and night. She no longer cared about school, and her short stay in rehab didn't help either. She knew that she was a mess, and her future looked bleak. She just did not care about anything anymore. She was beginning to question whether or not suicide would be the answer. She thought, "There must be another way. There just has to be." With that thought she fell asleep remembering that sad time four years ago.

She was a happy go-lucky twelve-year-old girl without a care in the world. Sharon was the star pitcher of her softball team and was making all A's in her classes at school. Yes, she was even a star in her seventh-grade class. Sharon was always laughing and embraced life with gusto. She was known as a tomboy most of the time wearing her light brown hair in pigtails. Sharon got her looks and personality from her mother. But there were times that she didn't even mind being a girly-girl by wearing dresses and ribbons in her hair. But most of the time, it was t-shirts, blue jeans, and pigtails. Her bright blue eyes shined with the friendliness of her personality and soul. Simply put, Sharon was the perfect little girl. However, she wasn't the only child in the family. There was a little boy, four years old.

His name was Jason. Like Sharon, he also sported light brown hair, but he had his Daddy's eyes. They were hazel in color, almost green. Being a typical four-year-old, precocious and mischievous, he could be a handful. Sometimes Sharon would play with him, but there were times that she just wanted to be left alone. There were times when she just felt like screaming. He was always running into her room and messing up her stuff. "Why can't he just go away?" Sharon would learn to regret those very thoughts.

It was the summer just after her thirteenth birthday, and Sharon had invited a couple of her friends over to go swimming in the family pool. It was an above ground pool; nothing fancy. But it was just as fun as having an in-ground pool. They were splashing and having a grand ole time. Sharon's mom, Carol, had to run to the grocery store for a few items and did not want to take Jason. So, she asked Sharon if she could watch her brother while she was gone. Sharon was not too keen on the idea, but she just shrugged her shoulders and said OK. After Sharon's mom left, Jason came outside to where his sister and her friends were hanging out by the pool. They had finished swimming and were sitting in lawn chairs, drinking sodas, and soaking up the sun. Jason, being four, took it upon himself to climb the ladder leading up to the pool. Sharon hollered at him to get down. You see Jason was not allowed to go swimming alone because he had yet to take lessons. He climbed back down, found a floatation device, climbed back up again, and began to float around the pool. Sharon got up to check on him once, decided he was OK as long as he was using a floaty, and decided to go back and sit down with her friends. After about thirty minutes, Sharon did not hear any splashing around or anything. She jumped up from her chair to go check on her brother. What she saw next would cause her to go ghost white. Her brother was floating face down, not moving. Sharon shouted to her friends to call 9-1-1 while she was pulling her brother out of the pool. She tried to hit him, push him, and anything she could think of to help her brother breathe or at least move. When the paramedics and police arrived on the scene, it was already too late. One of the first responders, a police officer, was named John Morgan. He asked her where her parents were. Through her sobs, she told him that her mother had just gone to the store for a few minutes while her father was at work. Morgan wrote this down in his notebook that he carried. In the years to come, this notebook would help him solve a special challenging case.

Sharon was in hysterics and was fearful of what her mother and father would do and say. A few minutes later, Carol showed up from the store and panicked when she saw police and an ambulance. She immediately parked her car at a neighbor's house and ran to her own home screaming all the while. What she saw would make any mother's heart stop cold. Carol saw her precious little boy on a gurney covered up being wheeled into a coroner's vehicle. She then saw Sharon in hysterical tears. She ran to find out what had happened. At first police officers held her back, but when Sharon screamed for her mom, they let her go through. Carol ran to her little boy as she could not believe that he was dead. Sharon ran for her mother, but Carol pushed her away unknowingly. Sharon felt rejected and suddenly felt at fault. Carol grabbed for her little boy, but she had to be pulled away so the coroner could take his body for an autopsy. She fell to the ground sobbing profusely. Then for a moment, she seemed lucid. She had to get in touch with her husband.

Dan Foster was Construction Engineer and owned his own business. He started it out of his garage, and then the business took off from there. He had become a successful businessman. When he fielded the telephone call from Carol, the voice on the other end sounded frantic and hysterical, "Don," Carol frantically hollered, "Jason's dead! Jason's dead! He drowned in the pool." He was in the middle of a big negotiation with a high rise company to build condominiums. This contract would put Dan and his business in the book of Who's Who of the construction industry. When he learned of the news of his son, the strong, well-built thirty-five year old dropped the phone, sat down at his desk, and cried like a baby. He apologized to the gentlemen that represented the high-rise company and explained what had happened. He managed to reschedule the meeting for another date then rushed out the door telling his secretary that he had left for the day. He regained his control so he could drive home without incident. Over and over in his mind Dan was trying to make sense of it all. He had planned to take Jason under his wing when he was old enough and teach him the ropes of the company. All he could think of was how and why this happened.

Meanwhile, Carol walked over to Sharon who was still crying and shaking like a leaf. A paramedic was looking after her. She was told by the medic that Sharon needed to go to the hospital. Carol said that was OK and that she would ride with her. She then called Dan on his cellphone to let him know to meet them at Children's Hospital. Sharon kept looking at her mother saying, "I'm sorry; it's my fault. I checked on him; he seemed alright. I didn't know.... I didn't know...." She started crying again. Carol told her to calm down; that they would talk later. Carol could not believe what happened. She thought that she would wake up and find it all a nightmare. But in her heart, she knew it wasn't. Then it hit her like a ton of bricks. JASON WAS DEAD! He was never going to give her any more little boy hugs or blow kisses to her. He was never going to say, "Mummy, I wuv vu." He was never going to make those goofy little faces he liked to do when Carol was tired or feeling down. Just who was going to be her funny little clown now?

Her attention then turned to Sharon. Carol could not imagine what her daughter was going through or even what she thought when she saw her little brother not breathing. Carol's heart went out to

Sharon, but she herself was hurting. Would she ever be able to forget? And forgive? At that point in time, nothing made sense.

After Sharon woke up from her nap literally drained of emotion, she reflected back through the last four years. The whole family had to go through therapy. But then, Jason's room remained unchanged. The sign on his bedroom door was still there, "Jason's Room, Enter if you Dare." When you open the door, his bed was made all with his favorite stuffed animals on it. His clothes still hung in his closet. It was as if he was still living there. Kind of creepy in a way. Of course, both her parents forgave her, but the incident was still not forgotten.

Chapter Three

A Hopeful Day

For four years since the death of her brother, Shar, had been seeing a therapist. She and her parents sought therapy together, but it had been decided that Sharon continue her therapy sessions alone. For four years, she had not wanted to make new friends or participate in any school activities. She just sat in her room night after night, wanting to take back that fateful day. Sure there was a time that she thought her younger brother was a brat. But now, she would give or do anything to have him back. She would give anything for him to come in and mess up her room just one more time. If only she could go back in time and change things. Perhaps her parents would quit fighting and the whole household would be happy again. Her reasoning side of her brain told her that time travel was impossible. No one had done it, or it would be in the news. But could time travel be possible? Would life be so difficult if Jason did not drown? Shar started doing research on the computer but hit a stone wall there. Tomorrow at school, she would ask one of her few friends about this. For now, she saw a glimmer of hope.

The next day, Shar could not wait to get to school to talk to her friends. The first person on her list was her friend, Jonathan. He was, what you would call, a science nerd. Jonathan made 100s in Science, go figure. He probably would make Albert Einstein look lame. Even to look at him, no one would ever guess this. Jonathan usually wore black with earrings in his ears and sported a tattoo that said "Science Rocks." He was tall and lanky with long black hair that touched his shoulders. He looked more like a Goth kid than a science nerd. Shar cornered him in the court yard in front of the school before the first bell rang. About that time, another friend with short red curly hair walked up to greet them both. Wendy, Wen to her friends, dabbled in witchcraft. She hated the name Wendy. It reminded her of the old Casper cartoons where the female friend was named Wendy who was a witch and always flew around on a broom. Her hair was red as well. Along with the red hair, Wen had the most piercing green eyes. It was as if she could see right to a person's soul. She said the witchcraft that she experimented with was for good, but rumor has it that she may have been responsible for a curse or two. Anyway, Shar was so excited that she could not contain herself about her idea and strange notions about time travel. She asked Jonathon if it was possible. "Anything's possible," he said, "But no one has ever invented a machine. So far, it's just plain Science Fiction like <u>The Time Machine</u>. You know that kind of stuff. Why do you ask?" Shar told him that she wanted to travel back in time in order to keep her brother from drowning. He looked at her funny while asking, "are you sure that's a good idea? I mean, that's messing with the future or something like that. I don't know, Shar. That sounds kind of scary if you ask me. Remember when we had to read <u>A Sound of Thunder</u>?"

Wen, meanwhile, was intensively listening to this whole conversation. She simply said, "Yes, it is possible. I heard at a witch's counsel one time that a time portal could be conjured up. But it would have to be done by the high witches. You know, someone way up on the totem pole. However, I don't know if it has ever been tried." Shar looked at her with amazement, "could we find someone to do it? Please, Wen?" Wen said to her that they can ask her aunt after school. Wen's aunt, actually her great aunt, owned a magic shop. In the back of the store were items that only witches used, such as roots, frogs, etc. Wen knew that her aunt would be the one to ask. Shar seemed hopeful and for the first time in four years was actually happy. It was this notion that set the stage for the re-entry of now

Detective John Morgan into Sharon's life. Sharon had no idea of what kind of consequences that were going to ensue. She just wanted harmony back into her family. She and Wen made plans to go the magic shop after school. They asked Jonathon if he wanted to tag along. He said that he had plans and really did not want to dabble in the supernatural arts. Science was his thing. His philosophy was that there is a reason for everything and anything.

Chapter Four

THE WITCH

Wen's Aunt Serena was not a high witch or Wiccan, as they like to be called, but she knew who was. Being a Wiccan was not a bad thing as long as one did not practice the black arts. Serena occasionally would sell a love potion or conjure up small spells such as temporary amnesia especially when creditors would call her time after time. One time Serena, when she was younger, placed a spell on an ex-boyfriend who kept bugging her. He contracted strep throat and was laid up in bed for almost two weeks. Was it the spell or was it a coincidence? No one really knows. She wasn't your typical witch found on Halloween. There were no black, pointed hats in her wardrobe. The only time she would use a broom was to sweep her house with. She also did not go around saying, "Bubble, bubble. Toil and Trouble." She left that to the witches of Shakespeare's Macbeth. Yes, her hair was long but not black. She was beautiful with her long gray hair. She did wear a caftan for the customers. It seems that they expected something like that. But other times, no one could even pick her out in a crowd. However, there was a look of wisdom about her, not wrinkles but a look as if she knew numerous things about the universe.

When school ended, Wen and Shar walked to Serena's store which was not too far from the high school which opened for business one year prior. Since the house was a two story, Serena used the upstairs for living quarters. Wen would often visit her favorite aunt, so when she walked in the shop, Serena was not surprised. She was, however, interested in why Wen brought a friend. When the girls walked into the shop, it had an antique feeling with a musty odor. There were top hats, magic wands, playing cards, and all kinds of magic stuff. Oftentimes, this was the place where you could find a few boys from the elementary school. After all, magic was a subject that interests children of all ages. But for some reason, young boys were always attracted to this strange phenomenon of life. There was also a place in the corner where a small round table with four chairs stood. This was where customers could sit and enjoy a cup of Serena's special tea that she made. They all sat down at the table, and Shar told Serena about the circumstances surrounding her brother's death and her idea of returning to the past. But the girls did not come to drink tea; they came for answers.

Stroking her long gray hair, Serena leaned back in her chair and sighed, "I don't know, girls. Are you sure you want to do this? This action could take you down an extremely dangerous road. Remember what is done in the past can definitely affect the future." Shar looked seriously into Serena's eyes and calmly said, "Yes, I'm sure. More than you know." Wen looked pleadingly at her aunt and simply said, "Please." Serena stood up and said, "OK. Let me see what I can do, and I'll get back to you in about three days." Serena knew what this entailed and who she would have to contact. She was doubtful of this and thought best against it. But Sharon was not thinking of any repercussions as she thought, "one step closer, one step closer." She kept thinking about different scenarios concerning her family and how happiness would finally be restored. With that thought in mind, she walked the rest of the way home as if she was on cloud nine.

Chapter Five

THE FIRST VICTIM

John Morgan and Shelley Anderson poured over forensic notes and even took the elevator down to the basement of the Dallas Police Department to talk to the Medical Examiner. Since their squad made its home on the third floor of the Police Department, they had a chance to summarize what they knew about the case. They both knew that the victims were young women in their 20s, had light brown hair with blue eyes. Maybe somewhere in all of this information, they could catch a break before another murder took place. Dr. Charles DeWalt, M. E. for Dallas County for thirty years, buzzed them in as they approached the morgue. The aging doctor, who still acted like he was in his prime, proceeded to show x-rays and examiner notes to both detectives. He pointed out that each of the victims had similar markings on their wrists, feet, and neck. This was suggested that they were tied up and strangled. The knife wounds were made postpartum (after death). There were exactly four of them made on each victim, one in the heart, two in each lung, and the final blow was in the head or brain. Each mark was made in the exact same location and was made by the same knife. This bit of information proved that there definitely was a serial killer, and he/she made it personal. Now they had to start digging and find out who this sadistic killer is and stop him or her from another murder.

Morgan looked at Anderson and said, "This guy really did not like these women, or perhaps he was targeting one in particular." Anderson concluded by saying, "maybe we need to look at the families again and see what the common thread is besides physical appearance."

So, they took the elevator back upstairs to the squad room to look over the files again. The files had names and addresses of the ten murdered women. The first stop was the family of the first victim, Vicki Johansen.

Vicki was a student at the local community college and still lived with her parents. They lived humbly in a three-bedroom one story house. Mr. Johansen earned his living by being a postal worker, and Mrs. Johansen was a home health care provider. They were not rich by any means but lived comfortably. Since it was a Saturday afternoon, the detectives found the Johansens working outside in their yard. The couple looked to be in their early fifties and sported healthy physiques. They both ran marathons and finished races although neither of them came in the top ten. The husband and wife stopped what they were doing when Morgan and Anderson drove up. Out front under a huge pecan tree, there was a grouping of lawn furniture for them to sit down on. The interview began with Morgan asking both the Johansens about their daughter's social life.

"Was there anyone in Vicki's life who wanted to harm to her?" asked Morgan. Mr. Johansen calmly said, "No. Vicki was loved by everyone she knew. She had such a kind soul. Who would do such a thing?"

Shelley jumped in and asked, "Did Vicki have a boyfriend?" Mrs. Johansen answered that question as she briefly looked at her husband. "There was one guy who we both thought was a little flaky." "Really"? Morgan questioned. He then proceeded to remove a notebook from his jacket pocket to take notes. "What was his name, and why did you think he was flaky?"

"Well," Mr. Johansen said, "he started out to be a real nice kid, but then he started being obsessive and possessive. I mean; he threw a fit when he was not invited to our niece's wedding. He told Vicki that she could not go even though she was the maid-of-honor. One day, she had blonde highlights put in her hair. He immediately ordered her to change it back." Mr. Johansen looked at his wife and asked, "What was his name, honey?" Mrs. Johansen thought a moment and said, "Jason something. Jason Foster. That's it!"

Morgan looked up from his notepad and then back down again. He kept thinking that there was something familiar about that name but could not put his finger on it. He shrugged if off, then he and Shelley left the Johansen's house telling them that they would be in touch if anything comes up. For some reason, the name, Jason Foster, kept haunting him. He knew this name from somewhere, but where, he did not know. They then decided to interview the second victim's family hoping that there would be a connection.

Chapter Six

THE SECOND VICTIM

Back at the precinct again, Morgan pulled the file containing information about the second victim. These cases just seem to get stranger and stranger to him, and yet the name Jason Foster still haunted him. Janice Hill was a 20-year-old hostess at the local Olive Garden Restaurant who was working her way through college. She had dreams of becoming an elementary school teacher. She lived with her single mother in Mesquite, Texas. She was the second victim. Like Vicki, Janice also had light brown hair with blue eyes. Coincidence? Maybe, or maybe not!

Anderson volunteered to call Janice's mother so they could get a chance to talk with her about her daughter. They all agreed to meet where Ms. Hill worked. As it turned out, she was employed at Macy's at Town East Mall. They met at the food court on the third floor of the mall during Ms. Hill's lunch hour. Morgan could see where Janice had received her good looks. Connie Hill looked more like Janice's sister than her mother. Her gray-streaked brown hair streamed down the middle of her back while her blue eyes sported a pair of glasses resembling what John Lennon used to wear. At this point, the two detectives were hoping for a connection; something that would help bring this case together.

Morgan and Anderson were just finishing lunch when Ms. Hill approached their table and sat down. She immediately said, "I'm so glad that someone is finally looking into Janice's death. How can I help?"

Morgan again got his notebook from the inside pocket of his jacket. He began taking notes while Anderson started the interview. "Do you know of anyone that would want to harm Janice?" The answer given was similar to what the Johansens had given. Ms. Hill told the detectives, "Janice was everyone's friend. That's one reason why she was hired at The Olive Garden as hostess. She was a friendly girl, not a harsh word for anyone." Shelley continued, "did she have a boyfriend whom she may have had an argument with or perhaps a co-worker or customer?" Ms. Hill cupped her chin in her hand and thought for a moment, "Janice did mention that at one time there was a disagreement with a waiter concerning tips, but I dismissed it at the time. Do you think there's a connection?" Morgan then piped in and asked, "Did she mention a name?" Ms. Hill quietly answered, "Why, yes she did. His name was Jason, but I don't know his last name." Morgan closed up his notepad and put it back into his jacket pocket. "Thank you, Ms. Hill. We'll keep in touch." As Morgan and Anderson walked through the mall, they walked in silence as if digesting what they had just heard. After they both got into the car, Morgan suddenly said, "Do we need to interview the rest of the families?" Shelley looked at Morgan and said, "Maybe we need to interview the last victim's family just to make sure that we have a handle on this case. Then we need to talk to this Jason kid and his family." Morgan just nodded his head up and down in agreement and then started the car. Shelley then commenced dialing on her cell phone to make an appointment to see the most recent victim's family. Shelley secured a time to talk to the family later on that evening. She asked Morgan, "do you think it would be a good idea to revisit the crime scene where the last victim was found since we don't know where the original crime scenes took place?" Morgan said that it wouldn't hurt to take another look. So they both headed towards South Dallas to the wooded area where the bodies were found. Crime Scene Investigators had already combed the area for evidence with little success. Hopefully two trained detectives could put a different perspective on things. Sometimes different eyes can spot things that CSI could not.

Each body was found near the other one as if the killer was showing consistency and organization in a sick kind of way. Morgan thought that the place the killer chose was a place where he would go to think things out, a sort of serenity kind of place, where he felt at home. As Morgan and Anderson were walking through the woods, they came upon a stream. It gave Morgan a kind of tranquil feeling as if he himself would go to. Anyway, after bending down and going under the Crime Scene tape, they both started looking for anything that stood out, not a part of the environment. Just as they were about to give up, something glittered in the sun. It was about a hundred feet away to Morgan's left. He walked over to it and shouted to Anderson, "I think I've found something here!" Shelley walked over to where he was and looked down to what Morgan had found. It was a knife! As Morgan put on his surgical gloves and picked up the knife, he shook his head and said, "how in the world can the Crime Scene Lab folks miss this? It wasn't hidden. I don't get it." Shelley said, "I don't know, but here we are. Finally, a piece of evidence that can be helpful. Here, put it in this plastic bag. Hopefully, some DNA or finger prints can come off of this." As Morgan and Anderson walked back to the car, they discovered some pieces of cloth left on a shrub as if someone had their shirt or jacket torn as he/she was walking through the woods. They bagged this too. Morgan said, "We'll get these items back to the lab ASAP and then go see the family of the last victim. I have a feeling that this case is getting closer and closer to being solved.

Chapter Seven

THE REQUEST

Serena, Wen's aunt, sat at her antique roll top desk flipping through her Rolodex file of phone numbers. There were numbers that she did not keep archived in her cell phone. These were numbers that belonged to members of her Wiccan coven. She plucked five numbers from the Rolodex and began calling the people to whom the numbers belonged. Her first contact belonged to Phillip who was considered the high priest of the coven. In the real world, Phillip was CEO and president of a large grocery store chain. He kept his religion a secret from his co-workers; however, it was his religion that contributed to his success. He stood six-foot with an athletic build and was anticipating the celebration of his 50th birthday. Despite his age, Phillip's sandy blond hair and piercing green eyes made him look thirty. He never married, and it seemed that every single-statused female in the coven harvested a secret crush on him. But Phillip was all business. He was either busy with his company or preforming various Wiccan duties. Either way, he had no time for relationships and preferred it that way.

When Phillip answered the phone, he was surprised to hear Serena's voice on the other end. After all, she rarely called him except for extreme important matters. After saying 'hello', Phillip asked Serena what the matter was. Serena asked in a nonchalant manner, "What is the protocol for conjuring up a time portal?" Phillip, sounding a little skeptical, answered, "Why do you ask? You know that we don't do that anymore. The coven decided years ago that it was simply too dangerous to mess with the future. Do you not remember what happened the last time we did this?" Serena said, "I know, but this is an urgent manner and could mean the difference between a young teen committing suicide and living a satisfying life." Still sounding hesitant, Phillip said, "We need to meet with the elders and the person requesting this in order to vote on whether or not it would be sanctioned." Serena calmly said, "I understand. It shall be done. When and where do we meet?" Phillip said, "I will call the elders today and have a meeting next Thursday evening at the sound of the sixth bell (meaning 6 pm). We will also need to refer to **"The Book of Shadows." The Book of Shadows** is a book containing religious texts and instructions for magical rituals found within the religion of Wicca. Serena answered, "OK. I will contact the party involved. We will be there next Thursday. Thanks, Phillip." They both said goodbye. After hanging up the phone, Serena put the remaining phone numbers back into her Rolodex as she knew that Phillip would make the necessary phone calls.

With a disconcerting thought, Phillip started making the calls to the elders. The first call Phillip made was to Clark Williams who eventually will step up and take over Phillip's position as high priest. Clark was in his mid-thirties, had coal black hair with dark brown eyes. Even though Clark was a bit young to be an elder, he inherited his position from his mother upon her death. Clark was an Afro-American whose roots go back to Africa. His great-great grandfather was chieftain of an African tribe before being abducted and sold into slavery. Clark's occupation at the time was that of a construction engineer. He owned his own business and was extremely successful. You see, all members of Phillip's coven were successful not only professionally but in everything else.

When Clark answered the phone with Phillip on the other end, he was not surprised.

"Clark," said Phillip. "We need to call a meeting of the elders." Clark asked, "Why? What's up?" After a few seconds but what seemed like hours of silence, Phillip told Clark about a time portal being requested to be conjured up. Clark said forebodingly, "Phillip, you can't be serious. You know what happened last time we did this!" Phillip simply said, "I know, but Serena said it was important. We'll meet next Thursday evening at six to discuss it further." "OK," said Clark, "but I just want you to know that I think it is a bad idea. See you next week." After the good byes were said, Phillip proceeded to call the remaining elders.

The remaining three were: Patricia Cortez, a 42-year-old Latino divorcee who owned a floral shop; Jennifer Jones, a 44-year-old elementary school teacher; and Charles Schmidt, a 52-year-old with a German accent who was a professor at the local community college. With each phone call made, Phillip sat down on his leather couch and reflected on the disapproval that each of the elders projected. He sat in silence anticipating just calling Serena and telling her "NO." But he had yet to hear the reason for such a request. He would just have to wait until the following Thursday.

Serena, after hanging up from talking with Phillip, then called Wen to give her the information about the meeting. Wen then proceeded to call Sharon with the news. Sharon was so hopeful that her days were filled with happiness. Her mood was more positive and uplifting. Even her parents noticed it and commented on her behavior of late. She even shared the news with her friend, Jonathan. He was, of course, still skeptical.

The days went by what seemed to be forever. Finally, Thursday came. Sharon made sure that she was dressed accordingly. She definitely wanted to make a good impression. Since her wardrobe consisted mostly of Gothic attire, she decided to borrow one of Wen's dresses. It was a nice floral print which helped to highlight Shar's blue eyes. Feeling confident, she and Wen drove to Serena's house and left from there to the meeting.

As Phillip's cuckoo clock announced the time being 6:00pm, all parties concerned started to arrive. They were each shown to a basement door of which there were stairs leading down to the basement which housed a special meeting room made just for the coven. In Texas, basements were rare due to the constant shifts of the ground causing foundation problems, but this basement was specially built. In the middle of the room stood a large circular table made of mahogany wood with twelve chairs surrounding it. It kind of looked like King Author's round table for his knights. Just five feet away stood a locked display case with four shelves which housed not only **The Book of Shadows** but also some Wiccan paraphernalia. All around the room were candles of different sizes lit to give the room a certain ambiance. The elders sat at one end of the table with Phillip in the middle while Serena, Wen, and Shar sat at the other end. Phillip, wearing a flowing white robe, stood and addressed Serena, "Since you are here on the behalf of young Sharon Foster, please tell the elders what her request is, and why we should grant it." Serena, sounding serious as Phillip, simply said, "Sharon, or rather Shar, requests a time portal to be opened, but, in my opinion, Shar can explain better than me as to what the reason is." Phillip sat down and directed his speaking towards Shar, "This is highly unusual, but go ahead and proceed. Tell us why in the world would we want to conjure much less consider a time portal."

Shar anxiously started speaking rapidly as she was nervous as a caught fox in a hen house. Phillip instructed her to take a deep breath and slow down. She gingerly started over telling the story about her brother, Jason, and the situation at her home. She further explained what her life had been like within the past four years. Pleadingly,

Shar continued to convince the elders that if she could go back in time to save Jason, the lives of her family would be better. Phillip and the other elders suggested that Serena and the girls wait upstairs in Phillip's living room while they discussed Shar's request. The living room, like the basement, was massive and luxurious. There were antiques and plush sofas present. Shar and Wen were almost hesitant to sit on any of the furniture. The waiting seemed to last forever. Everyone sat in silence wondering what the outcome would be.

Thirty minutes later or what seemed to be longer, Jennifer left the basement room and ascended the stairs to announce that the elders had made a decision. She led them all back downstairs. Serena and the girls resumed their seats that they occupied earlier. Phillip again stood up and addressed the trio. He said, "Against my better judgment, we are prepared to open a time portal; however, we will never speak of this again. This will take place in two weeks during the full moon at exactly midnight at our ceremony site. The only people that will be allowed to attend will be the members of the coven and you two girls. Is that understood?" Shar grinned and said, "Absolutely!"

As Serena and the girls left Phillip's house, Shar's spirits flew higher than a kite. She had not felt this euphoric since she was on drugs. So now she knew what a natural high felt like. Serena gently tugged on her and told both girls, "No one, and I mean No one is to know of this night or what was discussed. Is this clear?" They both agreed. But Shar turned to Wen and asked, "So, we can't even tell Jonathan, Mr. Doubtful?" Wen said, "No. No one, Shar. We'll get into trouble if we do. So, mum's the word. You understand." Shar nodded yes, but secretly she had wished that she could tell the world.

Chapter Eight

THE EVIDENCE

Back at the squad room, Morgan and Anderson poured over their notes. The name Jason Foster kept haunting Morgan's memory. There was something about that name he could not let loose. Maybe it was related to an old case. He would have to thumb through his old notebooks. All of a sudden, the shrill of his telephone startled him back to reality and the present. When he answered it, the forensics lab was on the other end. Ronnie Stevens, who was a forensics wiz kid, told Morgan that he had some good news. Dallas was lucky to hire Ronnie as he graduated top in his class at MIT but also held a degree in Criminal Forensics. The twenty-five-year-old red head from Virginia was probably one of the biggest assets that the Dallas Police Department had on staff. The evidence that he found from what Morgan and Anderson found in the empty field would help Morgan to put a lid on this case. Anyway, both detectives took the elevator down to the 1st floor where the forensics lab was housed. As they left the elevator, the aroma of alcohol entered their nostrils. It reminded Morgan why he did not venture down here too often. The whole floor was dedicated to forensics whether it is DNA, blood type, or bullet testing. There were microscopes for viewing slides and even electron microscopes for all those intricate tests that needed to be done. The larger items to be scanned for evidence such as cars, etc. were kept in a garage on the ground floor. There were at least a dozen men and women in white lab coats looking like a busy bee hive. Hustling here and there, the scientists seemed not to pay attention to Morgan and Anderson as they arrived. About that time, Ronnie walked up to them and told them to follow him to his lab area. He had something important to share.

At first glance, his lab area looked to be cluttered, but Ronnie knew where everything was placed. He had bags of evidence; each was labeled with a victim's name on it along with a date and the content description. First, he reached for the knife that Morgan found in the wooded area where the bodies had been found. Ronnie had managed to find some latent fingerprints by using super glue fumes. The fumes, when heated in a specialized container, were able to lift the prints. He then placed fingerprint tape over the handle of the knife and ran it through AFIS (Automated Fingerprint ID System) which is a data base that stores thousands of fingerprints. If a person had a police record, this is where the name would be stored by using fingerprints. He told Morgan and Anderson that he found a match. At no surprise to Morgan, the fingerprints matched up with none other than one Jason Foster. Ronnie further told the detectives that he was able to find traces of blood on the blade of the knife. It matched to the latest victim, Jennifer Robinson. Now they had a name to the unknown suspect. They had evidence that put the knife in his hands and proof that he had used it on the last victim. Morgan asked Ronnie to run a DMV (Department of Motor Vehicles) check to see what the latest address was for this charming fellow. After talking with Jennifer's family, the two detectives would make an attempt to seek some background information on Jason and try to find him.

Chapter Nine

THE TENTH VICTIM

Jennifer Robinson made her living as a cocktail waitress off of lower Greenville Avenue. This section of the street was well known for the local college crowd mainly where they would do their partying. There were also restaurants mixed in with the bar scene. However, Jennifer was waitressing while attending college at the same time. She also lived in a rent house not too far from where she worked so all she had to do was walk to work. Her parents, Martha and Paul Robinson, lived in a Lake Highlands addition not too far from this well crowded area was. They were both worried about their daughter living in this area. One would never know just what a drunken college student would do especially in a crowd.

Morgan and Anderson arrived at the Robinson house and were impressed by the size of the house. The two-storey structure included a two-car garage, a fenced yard, and an in-ground swimming pool. Needless to say, whatever Paul Robinson did for a living, he brought home a pretty good sized pay check. Morgan knocked on the door after looking around making sure to see if someone was home or not. Loud barking from the other side of the door could be heard. From what he could gather, the barking belonged to a large breed of dog. As the door opened, a small framed woman of oriental decent was holding back a large yellow Labrador Retriever. Morgan flashed his badge and asked if he and Anderson could come in and talk with the Robinsons. Yokima, as she was later to be known, told them to wait while she put the dog outside. When she returned to the front, she opened the door and led them inside. As the two detectives walked in the house, they could not help but admire the furnishings. The inside was just as impressive as the outside. The housekeeper showed them to a formal living room which was furnished with Louis XIV furniture. She also told the detectives to wait until Mrs. Robinson could join them. Morgan almost didn't want to sit down for fear that he might mess it up. As Mrs. Robinson entered the room and sat down, she motioned for the two to do likewise. Morgan reaching inside his jacket retrieved his notebook in order to write down notes.

Morgan asked Mrs. Robinson if her husband was at home. She replied that he was working late and could not meet with them as scheduled. She was all business and was soon asking questions about her daughter's death. "Have you caught the killer yet? Do you know who it is? Is it male or female? Detectives, please give me something, so my husband and I can find some kind of closure." Morgan was taken aback somewhat. After all, he was the one that was supposed to ask the questions. He told her, "We have not arrested anyone, yet. But we have new evidence that has given us a clue as to who it might be. But first I need to know if Jennifer, to your knowledge, has had anyone threaten her or bother her in anyway. Did she have a boyfriend, maybe, with whom she had a quarrel?" Mrs. Robinson quickly rose from the couch from where she was sitting and walked over to the mantel where the fireplace was then picked up a picture of her daughter. Morgan could not help but see again the resemblance of the other victims, brown hair and blue eyes. The lady of the house then turned around and said, "Detective Morgan, now those are interesting questions. Jennifer was so popular throughout high school and even pledged a sorority at college. She believed that it would look good on a resume. She was studying to be an architect, a career primarily held by men. But this is what she wanted, so my husband and I encouraged her. Now, back to your questions. There was this one person that briefly worked at the bar as a bartender where Jennifer worked. He was always giving her grief about one thing or the other. I simply told her to ignore him and report him to the owner of the bar." While Morgan was writing all this new information down, Anderson asked her, "Mrs. Robinson, would the name of this person happen to be Jason Foster?" Mrs. Robinson's eyes grew big when she exclaimed, "Why, yes it was! Why? Is he the one? Did he kill my precious Jennifer?" "We believe so, Mrs. Robinson. By the way, do you remember the name of the bar where Jennifer worked?" "Why, yes. I do believe that the bar was called The Glass Slipper. I do hope you get this guy and put him away forever." Morgan and Anderson got up and told Mrs. Robinson thank you for the information and that they would let themselves out. Morgan turned to Anderson when they got outside and said, "I guess our next step is to talk with the family and then go get this guy before there is a number eleven." Anderson nodded her head in agreement. "Let's go get this creep. He sure has my dander up. I would just love to see the needle go in his arm." With that remark, Anderson and Morgan proceeded to get into their squad car in the direction of the foster house.

Chapter Ten

THE RITUAL

As the hour was reaching midnight on the clock, Phillip made sure that he had all his tools for the ritual. He had gathered four candles each representing the four directions on a compass. He also carried with him some matches, salt, water, and ceremonial bowls. But before he gathered up all the necessary tools for this ceremony or ritual, he had consulted the **Book of Shadows** for the spell that was needed. He quickly wrote down the words and instructions as he wanted everything to be perfect. One false slip, the whole spell could go wrong and no telling what would happen. The last thing he gathered up was his white robe. After all, how can a high priest conduct a ritual or ceremony without it? The only reason he wore it was to remind his coven that he is the high priest until his death. Now that he had everything, Phillip was out the door and in his Jaguar in a manner of minutes. The ceremony site was thirty minutes out of town located in a highly wooded area. There were no signs or markings of any kind, but all the members in the coven knew where to go.

Normally, each Wiccan would conduct their own ceremonies in the privacy of their own homes, but on occasion, the twelve members would gather together for something special, such as a birth, a wedding, or a funeral. Tonight, this was to be an extra special ceremony, more like a ritual. Phillip still had misgivings concerning the reason behind this ritual, but he understood. He came upon a dirt road that seemed to head nowhere. Large trees loomed over the road making it look like a tunnel. It was so dark, Phillip needed to use his bright lights of his car just to meander his way to the ritual site. When he arrived, there were a few of his coven members already present. The pentagram had been laid out with stones exactly done just like in the medieval period and ever since. Alters were set up for the ritual bowls that would represent the natural elements of water, fire, earth, and air. There were also podiums set up for the four candles which would be facing north, south, east, and west. As Phillip began placing bowls and candles on the podiums, the rest of his members arrived including Serena. Wen and Shar had followed Serena in Wen's car, a sixteenth birthday present from her parents. The cars were parked in a semi-circle so some of the headlights could be used in order to see. This place was perfect because no one knew where it was, and no one bothered them. Phillip was still concerned about allowing an outsider witness such a ritual. This was to be sacred, and secrecy was a must. He then instructed his coven to hold hands and form a circle surrounding the pentagram. Then the ritual began.

Phillip instructed Shar to go into the middle of the circle. He gave her a piece of paper and told her to hang onto it for life. He said, "say this only when you are ready to return. You must return when the deed is done, not too soon and not too late. Understand?" She said nervously,

"Yes, sir. I understand." Nervous was an understatement.

She was downright scared. Shar had no unearthly idea what was going to happen. None whatsoever. With this done, Phillip started the incantation:

> *"Goddess of the East, of the West, of the North, of the South, we ask your blessing. We call to you to witness and to guard this circle and all within it. Powers of air and water, of fire and of earth, travel with Shar now as she travels to the past."*

As Phillip was chanting, he started swaying, and the coven, while holding hands, was also swaying from left to right with their eyes wide open as if in a trance. Phillip then instructed Shar to repeat after him, "I wish to go back; back toward the past; back to when I was 13; back in the summer when my brother drowned." Shar then repeated the exact words, and Phillip looked to the heavens and shouted as he closed the incantation with, *"Wind, Fire, Water, Earth, I call on you to make this spell magic! So mote it be!"*

All of a sudden, the wind began to swirl, and the leaves on the ground began to whirl. A dark blue tunnel loomed above Shar and engulfed her. It then disappeared as well as her. The coven then stopped swaying, and the circle was broken. Wen whispered to her Aunt Serena, "how long do we wait?" Serena shushed her, "as long as it takes." Phillip then simply asked, "Who brought the snacks?"

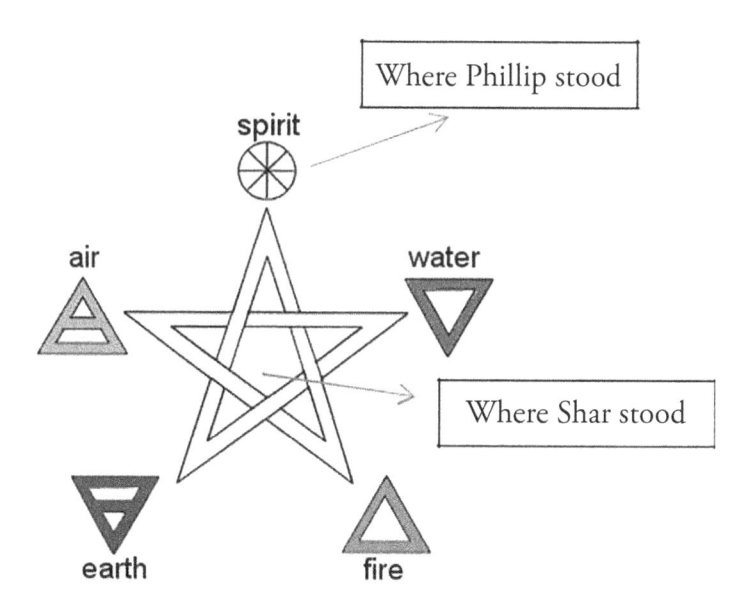

Chapter Eleven

THE SAVE

Before Shar knew it, she was back at her house. Thoughts raced through her mind, "funny, it doesn't look any different. What if the spell didn't work? Now what? But wait a minute. It's daylight. Maybe? Could it be? Perhaps it did work after all."

Shar found herself in the kitchen looking outside. No one was there yet, so she walked upstairs to where the bedrooms were located. She heard giggling in the bathroom and knew that her younger self as well as her friends were in there. She reached into the left-hand side of her jacket and found the notes which she wrote earlier this evening. Shar had been instructed to not talk or contact her younger self in any way or the spell would be broken, and she would return immediately to the present. She was glad that she had told her parents that she was spending the night with Wen. She softly walked into the bedroom and placed one note on the student desk and the other one in the pocket of the swimsuit cover up that her younger self would wear that day. She then slipped out and slowly went back downstairs. It was that moment when her younger self entered the bedroom.

The thirteen-year-old Sharon walked over to the bed and found her cover up and put it on, but then something caught her eye that was on her desk. It was a note of some sort. Funny, she didn't remember it being there before. She walked over to the desk and picked it up to read it. "SAVE HIM; HE WILL DROWN." It wasn't signed or anything. She thought it was a joke by one of her friends, laughed to herself, wadded the paper up, and threw it away. Sharon then rejoined her friends, walked downstairs, opened the back door, proceeded to dump towels on the lawn chairs, and go swimming. Shar winced at this particular action but then still had hope with the second note.

Carol, her mother, opened the door just to holler at Sharon to watch her little brother while she ran up to the store for a few minutes. Shar was standing near the back door. She was told by Phillip that no one would be able to see her. That's the way time travel worked. Also, she was NOT to interfere in any way. In other words, she herself could not save Jason. If there was to be a change, it would have to be instigated by the younger Sharon. Reluctantly, young Sharon agreed to watch Jason. She went to take off her cover up and again found a note in one of the pockets. She opened it up and silently read it. It read, "SAVE HIM; HE WILL DROWN." She turned to her friends and asked, "Ok, this is not funny; who wrote this?" Both of them looked at the note and said, "I didn't do it. Not my handwriting." Sharon knew it wasn't her mother's handwriting. She knew that handwriting by memory. After all, she forged it one time. "So, who wrote it?" she thought. She still thought it was some sort of sick joke and dismissed it. The sixteen-year-old Shar stood by nervously waiting to see what would happen. It took all the willpower she had not to go running out and save her brother herself.

After the girls finished swimming and were sitting in the lawn chairs, Jason came bounding out in his four-year-old style heading for the pool. Sharon remembered the notes and hollered at Jason, "Jason, mom said not to go swimming alone." "I'm not. You're out here." "You'd better mind, buster, or I'll tell mom." "Oh, ok." But Jason, being the mischievous four-year-old that he was, tip toed back outside, grabbed a flotation, and went into the pool. Sharon heard splashing and thrashing around then all went silent. She ran over to see what was going on. She saw her brother lying face down in the pool. She yelled to one of her friends to go call 9-1-1 and to the other one to come help her. She then climbed into the pool, grabbed her little brother, and carried him to her friend. After hoisting him out of the pool, she put him flat on the ground and started CPR (cardio pulmonary resuscitation). All of a sudden, Jason started coughing and spewing up water. Then he started crying. About that time, an ambulance and a police car arrived. The EMTs (Emergency Medical Technician) checked Jason out and decided that he would be OK, but he needed to go to the hospital just to be checked out. About that time Carol arrived and ran over to her children to see what had happened. After talking to the police and finding out what had happened, she walked over to her daughter and hugged her while proclaiming her to be a hero. She then called her husband at work to swing by the house to pick up Sharon and meet them at the hospital as Carol would be riding with her son in the ambulance.

Shar, being satisfied that her mission was accomplished especially when her mother was already home from the grocery store, remembered the note in her pocket that Phillip gave her to use when she was ready. She was tempted to click her heels three times like Dorothy in the <u>Wizard of Oz</u>, but she didn't. She closed her eyes instead and began the incantation, "I wish to go forward in time back to where I said the first rhyme." Then the winds swirled and leaves whirled, then poof, she vanished. The next thing she knew she found herself on the ground back in the circle where it all began.

When she stood up, she noticed that she was not wearing black anymore, and her hair was not dyed black. In fact, she felt good, and a certain kind of happiness seemed to cover her up like a blanket. Wen came over to check on her and noticed the change in her. She quickly asked Shar, "What happened? Did it work? Shar, tell me everything!" "Wen, why are you calling me Shar? You know my name is Sharon." Wen said she was sorry but told Sharon how different she looked. She had a glow about her that was hard to explain. Sharon quickly asked Wen if they could leave then she would tell Wen all about it at her house. Wen said that they could not leave until Phillip gave the sign to do so. Phillip walked over to Sharon, Wen, and Serena. He said, "You must not ever speak of what happened here no matter what the outcome may be. Remember what you changed in your past will affect your present and most definitely your future." No one must ever know. No one! Is that clear?" They all agreed, but Sharon really wanted to share this experience with her parents, but she knew that she could not. Phillip then dismissed the coven, and everyone helped in gathering up the ritual bowls, candles, and other items. They gathered the stones and buried them just in case they would use them again. The podiums and alters were put into various trunks of the coven members so they could take them home and put them away. When the area was cleared, there was no evidence of anything that took place in the woods. Then one by one everyone was in their cars heading down the dirt path and home again. When Wen and Sharon got to Wen's house, they quietly climbed up the trellis near Wen's bedroom where they had climbed down. Sharon sat on Wen's bed and told her everything that had happened. She was so excited that she could not wait to go home and see if things were really different. After dressing for bed, she slept like a log, and it was the best sleep that she had had in four years.

Chapter Twelve

THE RETURN

The next morning which was Sunday, Sharon said her goodbyes to Wen and her family then rushed home. She didn't live too far so she was able to walk home with little effort. When she got to her house, she was just a tad nervous. After all, Sharon was not quite sure of what to expect. She retrieved her key from her backpack and unlocked the front door. She decided to just walk in as if there was nothing going on. She saw her father sitting in his reclining chair reading the Sunday paper as usual while her mother was in the kitchen cooking breakfast. Sharon stopped long enough to say good-morning then climbed the stairs up to her room. First, she stopped in front of Jason's room. That same sign was on his door. She quietly knocked then opened the door. Inside she saw what seemed to be a young boy approximately eight years old laying on his bed reading a comic book. Jason paused and looked up, "What do you want? Don't you believe in knocking?" "But Jason, I did knock. Besides I just wanted to say good-morning." He said, "Whatever. Uh, don't forget to close the door on your way out. Bye." Sharon could not believe what she saw and what she heard. But to her ears, it was like music. Her brother had survived. When Sharon opened the door to her own room, she could not believe what she saw. Did someone transform her room? Where were her gothic posters? When she put her backpack up in her closet, again there was a mystery staring at her. Where were her gothic clothes? Then she remembered what Phillip had said. The past would affect the present and the future. Sharon theorized that in this future, she was not depressed nor was she withdrawn and moody. That was why she felt an overwhelming happiness when she transported back from the past. The past had changed; therefore, her present had changed. Makes sense now. The rest of the day and evening went by normally. Sharon and her parents settled in to watch a DVD movie with sodas and popcorn. Jason was holed up in his room playing video games which was no surprise there. But even at dinner, Jason seemed a little off. He picked at his food and stared at his plate. He looked as if he was distracted by something, but what Sharon had no clue. She was just happy to see him alive.

The next morning, being Monday, Sharon hurriedly dressed for school in a crisp light green dress accessorized by white flats and dark green earrings. Just seeing all this stuff, what seemed new to her at this point, made her feel anew and even a tad adventuresome. She couldn't wait to see Wen, so she hurried downstairs, hugged her mother while she was cooking breakfast, and then walked over and gave her father a hug while he was reading the morning news. Jason had not made it down yet. Apparently, this was a ritual around the household. Dan Foster put down his paper, got up, walked over to the bottom of the stairs, and hollered up at Jason to hurry up or he just might miss the foster taxi to school. He slowly descended the stairs and sat down to eat his breakfast. This time Jason did manage to eat something without picking at it. He then ran back upstairs to retrieve his backpack which he forgot when he came down for breakfast. He then jumped down the stairs taking two at a time. I guess, Sharon thought, this was normal behavior for an eight-year-old. She shrugged it off and grabbed her own backpack which she placed at the bottom of the stairs when she came down. Then out the front door and into the car Dan and his children went. First stop was Jason's school. When Dan pulled up to the curb to let Jason out, some of Jason's friends, or so Sharon thought, were already gathered at the front door of the school. Jason quickly unbuckled his seat belt, climbed out of the car, and slammed shut the car door as Dan told him to have a good day. His father just rolled his eyes and said, "Kids, go figure." The next stop was Sharon's school, North Dallas High School. She would recognize that school anywhere. Nothing seemed to change – from the outside anyway. After unbuckling her seatbelt, Sharon reached over to her father and gave him a peck on the cheek. He asked, "What was that for?" She just simply said, "Because I love you, Dad." With that, she grabbed her backpack, got out of the car, and proceeded to walk the sidewalk leading up to the school but not before turning around waving goodbye to her Dad. He just smiled and drove on to work.

As she was ascending the steps up to the front door, Sharon saw her friends, Wen and Jonathan, and proceeded to meet them. There were several other students that said hello to Sharon which surprised her. Before the change, no one else gave her the time of day. Now everyone was friendly. She found out later on that even her grades had changed, for the better. Yes, her future seemed brighter and brighter.

Chapter Thirteen

JASON AND FAMILY

Detectives John Morgan and Shelley Anderson discovered the address of Jason Foster's parents after running DMV records on them. They still lived in North Dallas, not too far from the Galleria, a nice uptown mall, or so what Morgan thought. After retrieving notes and a file on this case from the precinct, they both headed over to interview Mr. & Mrs. Foster. They were also hoping to get some idea where Jason was. They lived off of Preston Hollow Road where several nice homes were. It took Morgan and Anderson about thirty minutes to arrive at the fosters' house. While they were in route, Anderson, who was not driving, called the Fosters to see if they were home. She received an affirmative answer from the other end of her cell phone.

The detectives pulled up to a house that made Morgan's three-bedroom look like chump change. It was a two-storey brick home with not two but three car garages. Morgan was wondering if there were actually three cars parked there. The lot itself was close to being one acre with large shade trees. The front of the house was something from <u>Gone With the Wind</u>. They both got out of the car and walked up the sidewalk which was surrounded by a landscape that looked like a picture right out of <u>Better Homes and Gardens</u>. Morgan rang the doorbell, and a nice-looking older woman opened the door. Mrs. Foster showed them into the living room which was massive. It was the size of Morgan's den and kitchen put together. Of course, Anderson was used to such luxury. After all, she was the daughter of the District Attorney and was used to such lavishness. Her father, before becoming the DA of Dallas County, had been a prominent criminal attorney.

As they sat down on the plush sofa, Morgan could not help but seeing pictures of their now grown children on the mantel of the stone fireplace. He could not help but think what great looking kids they are. Too bad one of them could be a possible bad seed. He also could not help but notice that the picture of their daughter was the smitten image of the murdered women in his file. He asked if Mr. Foster would be joining them. Carol told the detectives that he was on his way from work. Dan's business had grown to be one of the most prestigious commercial contractors in the Dallas-Ft. Worth area. This is why he could afford to live in the lap of luxury. As they were waiting, Carol offered the detectives either coffee or tea. They both chose coffee. By the time the coffee was made and served, Dan drove up and then soon joined his wife and the detectives in the living room.

As usual, Morgan retrieved his notebook from inside his jacket and began to write down notes as they interviewed the parents of the alleged murderer. Morgan opened his file on the coffee table in front of him and proceeded to show the two pictures of ten women.

"Do you know any of these women?" asked Morgan. "Dan said, "Why no. Should we?"
Anderson piped in and asked, "Where is your son, Jason?"

With downtrodden eyes, Mrs. Foster explained that they have not had contact with Jason for at least a year. Neither knew where he was living nor knew his phone number nor where he worked. Dan said, "We can give you the address and phone number of Sharon, his sister. Maybe she knows. But why do you want to see Jason?"

Morgan told him, "There is no simple way to explain this but to say that we believe that he is responsible for the death of these ten women." Carol started crying as if someone had just died. Dan tried to comfort her, but all he could do is shake his head from side to side. He simply said, "I'm not surprised. I knew there was something wrong going on during his last visit. He had always seemed distant and aloof, but we didn't really did not know why until he was nearly drowned at the age of four." Then it dawned on him. This was the same Jason that was saved by his sister so many years ago. Morgan was a beat cop then, and he was one of the first responders. It was all coming together now. Talk about a full circle. This was why this boy's name kept rattling his memory. Softly, Shelley Anderson asked Mr. Foster what happened. "Well," he began, "when he was rushed to the hospital, we were told by the emergency room doctor that Jason was lucky to be alive. However, his brain had been deprived of oxygen but for only a short period. We were told that there could be some problems, emotional and developmental. We really did not see any of the warning signs until he was in elementary school. That's when the behavior problems started. We had to put him in special education and start him on therapy sessions. By the time he got into Middle School, he was starting fights at school. But high school was the worst. We had caught him torturing and killing the neighborhood cats. We were at our wits end. We finally had him committed to a mental institution. When he was eighteen, he was released. He went to live in a halfway house and got a job. We have only seen him once a year at Christmas. I guess to get presents; I don't know. So, you see, Detective Morgan, I'm not surprised." After Carol Foster composed herself somewhat, she added, "He does keep in touch with Sharon. Even though he treated her like the devil, she was always nice to him. But what puzzles me is why would he kill these women that resemble his sister?" Anderson answered, "That's what we want to know. You both have been helpful in giving us some insight and background information. Thank you for Sharon's phone number and address. We are going to get in touch with her next. But please don't contact her until we have had a chance to talk to her first." They both agreed, and then the detectives were shown the door telling the parents that they would keep in touch. Morgan kept shaking his head while muttering, "Those poor people. They seemed so nice." After they both got into the car, they sat a minute to absorb what was just said to them about Jason.

While Morgan started the car, Anderson proceeded to use her cell phone to call Sharon Foster. She answered her phone on the second ring. "Hello. This is Sharon. May I help you?" Anderson identified herself and informed Sharon that both she and Morgan needed to talk with her concerning her brother. Sharon, being at work, told them that she could see them after work at her house at about six in the evening. After she hung up the phone, Sharon sat and stared at her computer to what seemed to be hours but was only a few minutes. She could not help but reflect what happened when Jason was four, when he was growing up, the events surrounding her when she was sixteen, and now. She also could not dismiss those words what Phillip had said to her all those years ago. "What happens in the past will affect the present as well as the future." Now she had to live with what was done even though she thought it was for a good reason at the time.

Chapter Fourteen

THE FINAL PIECE OF THE PUZZLE

The apartment in which Sharon Foster lived was a contrast to the lavish house in which her parents lived which she preferred. However, the apartment was located in a nice part of Dallas. Turtle Creek Apartments were nothing to sneeze at. The building was a high rise and located just up the street from The Turtle Creek Mansion, a ritzy restaurant that required reservations and a dress code.

Both detectives walked up to the front door and pushed a buzzer which operated an intercom manned by a security guard. The disembodied voice asked, "Who's there, and who did you come to see?" Morgan answered, "We're Detectives John Morgan and Shelley Anderson from the Dallas Police Department, and we have an appointment with Sharon Foster in apartment number 505." "OK. I'll ring her up. Hold on." A few minutes later, the voice told the detectives to come on in. At this point, Morgan grabbed one of the handles and pulled on the door. They both walked through and were met by the person of whom the voice belonged to. They flashed their badges and were allowed to proceed to the elevators. On the ride up, they both were discussing the security of the building. "Boy, do you believe this place?" "It must cost a bundle to live here." "Well, look where her parents live. I bet they help out." At this point the elevator opened, and they stepped out onto the fifth floor.

They then walked on the plush carpet and found number 505. It was like being in a fancy hotel, something Morgan had not experienced except for the time when he was a young cop and worked security on the side for the Hilton back in Los Angeles. Anderson rang the bell located to the right of the door. After what seemed to be five minutes, the door opened. Before them was the person of whom the picture on foster's mantel belonged. She smiled and showed them in her apartment. They all walked into the living room and sat down. Morgan noticed that the view out of the large plate glass window was of downtown Dallas. What a magnificent view! He then pulled out his oh-so-famous notebook so he could jot down notes from this interview. He began by informing Sharon that her brother is wanted for questioning involving ten murders and asked if she had been in touch with him.

Sharon looked at Morgan and turned a shade of white like a ghost. He thought that she was going to pass out. Anderson found her way to the kitchen and got Sharon a glass of water. After she took a sip, she nodded her head up and down and said, "I had a feeling that something like this would happen." "What do you mean?" Morgan asked. "Well, ever since I was sixteen years old, I had an odd feeling that Jason was not just right. I mean; he was so moody and withdrawn. I did not know then that he had suffered some kind of brain damage when he almost drowned." Sharon looked straight into Morgan's eyes and said, "I feel like I know you from somewhere, but I don't know where. Anyway, Jason used to catch the neighborhood cats and torture them. My parents started to take him to therapy, but after a CT scan of his brain, that's when it was discovered….an abnormality of his brain. The ability to distinguish between right and wrong was gone." Sharon then put her head in her hands and started crying. "This is all my fault. I just know it. If I had not done what I did, maybe all of this would not have happened." While Morgan was writing all this down, he asked her to explain. She said, "You won't believe me if I told you." He said, "Try me. I have heard it all." Anderson handed her a tissue, and Sharon wiped her eyes with it. "Ok, where do I begin?" "How about at the beginning."

Sharon proceeded to tell Morgan and Anderson what took place when she was sixteen and how she had gone back in time to have his younger brother saved from drowning. "Did you say that you went through a time portal? You actually went back in time? You know I'm finding this hard to believe. Now where can we find Jason? I'm sorry, but we will have to take him in for questioning." Sharon looked at them both with pleading eyes. "It is true!" "But," Morgan said, "I was there. I remember the EMTs loading him up in an ambulance. He was very much alive." "Yes, I know. I remember you now. However, you see, Jason was not supposed to have survived. Originally, he didn't, but I went back in time so he could be saved. Don't you see? If he had not been saved, all those women would still be alive today! You've got to believe me! I know I'm not crazy!" Morgan was still not convinced, but he'll give her the benefit of the doubt. "OK, let's just say I do believe you. How was this done and by whom?" "Here, I'll give you the name of my friend, Wendy. She'll put you in the right direction. She's a witch." Morgan and Anderson looked at each other then back at Sharon. "Are you kidding me?" asked Morgan. "A witch? Come on. What do you take me for? There's no such thing." Anderson pulled on Morgan's sleeve and said, "Yes, there is, John. One of my friends is one only he doesn't broadcast it. If what she says happens then we need to at least investigate it." Morgan took the piece of paper with the name and address of one Wendy Miller, witch. As they were leaving Sharon's apartment, Morgan stopped Anderson on the way to the car, "You really believe this stuff?" Anderson said, "Yes, I do. I have been to a coven gathering and witnessed a ritual. It's the real deal, John. It exists – witchcraft, that is." "Well, I guess we had better go see this Ms. Wendy and see what she's all about."

Chapter Fifteen

WENDY'S STORY

Wendy Miller had inherited her Great Aunt Serena's magic shop along with the rest of the items. Nothing had really changed in that store from so many years ago. However, there had been changes in the coven since that night when she was sixteen. She hadn't really thought or talked about that night until Sharon had called her and told her about the visit she had from the two Dallas detectives. Of course, Wendy had no unearthly idea that Sharon's brother, Jason, was up to no good. She wasn't even prepared to go down the road that eventually led to Sharon going back into the past using a time portal. Anyway, Phillip had Alzheimer's now and was unable to be the High Priest. So, that put Clark Williams at the head. The membership had grown, but everyone that was there that night was basically the ones who conducted private meetings. The rest was included when a large ceremony or ritual was necessary.

Morgan and Alexander pulled up in front of the house that originally was occupied by a Ms. Serena Miller but now by her niece, Wendy. Morgan and Anderson had no problems finding the place since they were told by Sharon that it was within walking distance from her old high school, North Dallas High. As they pulled up to the aging house, they could not help but see that the house had been overgrown with vines and was in bad need of a paint job. Morgan thought that it would make a perfect haunted house for Halloween. As they gently walked up to the porch which creaked with each board, a young woman met them at the door. She showed them inside and took them directly where the same table and chairs were that Aunt Serena had so many years ago. As Morgan and Anderson walked through the house, they both noticed the magic paraphernalia on bookshelves and countertops. There were also jars that housed different types of herbs, crystals, and what seemed to be freeze-dried frogs and other reptilian creatures. Morgan felt like he was in another world. Pretty weird stuff! They both proceeded to walk to the back of the shop and then sat down. Wendy made some herbal tea as they talked. Morgan did not beat around the bush. He immediately started spouting off questions. "You do know Sharon Foster, right?" Wendy nodded in agreement. "You do know why we are here, right?" She nodded again in agreement. "Well, is there any truth to what she has told me? You know, about this time travel stuff?" Wendy looked into his eyes and simply said with a sigh, "Yes, it is true." Morgan looked at her as if she were crazy, but deep down, he knew she wasn't. She placed the tea in front of her guests and then proceeded to discuss, in her words, what happened that day so long ago.

"To begin with, I just need to tell you that we were all sworn to secrecy by the then high priest, Phillip. But since this involves ten murders, I will tell you everything." Morgan flipped to a new page in his handy little notebook to begin writing down what was being said. "Of course, you know by now that Sharon wanted to go back in time in order to help save her little brother from drowning. We went to see my aunt who used to live in this very house. This is where it started, our journey, or rather her journey. We then met with Phillip and the then high counsel so she could give her proposal. At first the counsel was reluctant, but they finally agreed to help. When it was the first night of the full moon at that time, we travelled somewhere outside of Dallas for the ritual. It was so secluded and private that I probably could not tell you where it was or even if it is still there. At first, I even felt doubtful. I mean, come on, time travel? Really? But what I witnessed that night surely made me a believer that night. After the spell was chanted, we witnessed a swirling and twirling and bright lights. Sharon, who was standing in the middle of the ceremonial circle suddenly vanished. What seemed like forever but was only about an hour, she suddenly returned. She looked different plus her whole personality changed. I mean; she was a much happier person. She kept saying, 'It worked; it worked.' Now, Detective Morgan, what do you think?" As Morgan finished writing his notes, he asked her, "Do you know about Jason's brain injury and how it affected his behavior?" Wendy said, "I kind of knew that there was something not quite right with him after the day he was saved." "What do you mean?" inquired Morgan. Wendy continued to tell Morgan and Anderson that Jason was always moody and withdrawn. "He even turned Goth when he was just 12 years old. Then when he hit middle school, that's when the problems really mushroomed. Once he took a cat and wrapped rubber bands around its front paws and left them that way. The paws eventually fell off. Can you imagine the pain? He even took a stray dog and hung it just to see it flail around. I mean, this kid was psycho. He showed no remorse whatsoever." Morgan and Anderson looked at each other and just shook their heads in disbelief. He then looked pensive at Wendy and simply said, "We need to fix this. You know; make it right. We need to go back in time and keep the sixteen-year-old Sharon from saving her brother. I know it sounds sad, but it needs to be done. After all, there is a reason for everything. He drowned to keep these animals from being tortured and these women to live out their lives." Wendy agreed. "I will have to get hold of the high priest and request a conference with the elders. I will get in touch with you." So Morgan gave her a business card with his name and phone number on it. The two detectives then left. Anderson then asked Morgan as they both got into the car, "Do we proceed with trying to find Jason?" "No," said Morgan. "We will proceed as planned, go back in time, and unfortunately keep Sharon from saving her brother."

Chapter Sixteen

ANOTHER VISIT TO THE PAST

Until they have heard from Wendy, Morgan and Anderson decided to turn their attention to some of their other cases. It had not been three days when Morgan's phone rang. He had been deep in thought about another case when the sound jerked him back to reality. He picked the phone up and answered it. "Morgan here." Wendy announced herself and proceeded to inform Morgan when and where the council meeting will take place. "Do I need to be there?" Morgan asked. Wendy said both he and Shelley need to be present. Evidence needs to be proven as to why another trip back through time would be warranted. "When is this meeting going to take place?" Wendy said, "This coming Saturday at six o'clock in the evening." That was two days away. "You need to come to my house, and we will ride together. There is protocol that needs to be followed, and we must follow it if this is to take place." Morgan answered back, "Is there anything that I need to bring with me?" Wendy said, "Just bring whatever evidence you have to prove to the coven that another trip to the past is a must." Anderson then spoke up, "Do we need to tell Sharon what we are going to do?" Wendy said, "Sharon will be at this meeting. It is important that she approves of the action to take place. She, herself, cannot go back. It must be someone else to thwart her sixteen-year-old self. This will also be decided at the meeting." After Morgan hung up the phone, he looked at his partner and said, "Well, Shelley, you ready for this? I mean, this is probably the weirdest thing we have ever done. What are your thoughts about all this?" Shelley simply replied, "We gotta do what we gotta do no matter what it is. If we can pull this off, ten women will live as they were predestined to do. In fact, if this works, maybe we should be looking into some of our other cases. Maybe we can work with this high priest person." Morgan, looking at her pensively, said, "Maybe, we'll just have to wait and see how this pans out."

Two days passed at what seemed to be a snail's pace, but Morgan and Anderson kept busy regardless. As the clock in Morgan's car approached 5pm on Saturday, he found himself picking up Anderson from her house and then headed to Wendy's house. She was out front already waiting for them. Somehow, she already knew when they would come. As they were riding in the car on their way to the designated place, Wendy asked the duo if they were nervous about this adventure. They both concurred that they were but knew that his event was necessary.

They traveled down the same roads that Wendy and Sharon ventured out on so many years ago. Everything seemed the same – the roads, the trees, and even the sky. It was as if the years had not melted away.

The trio arrived early before the high priest arrived. The other members of the coven were already present, milling around and waiting. It had been decided ahead of time to meet at the ceremony site just in case approval was given to conjure up the portal. That way the spell could be chanted, and the time portal could be opened. After what seemed to be forever, Clark Williams, the now new High Priest, and his entourage arrived. If this meeting was held indoors, a pin could have been heard. Awkwardness was the understatement. Chairs were brought out from a van that belonged to one of the members and placed into a circle. Each member plus the trio in question stood in front of a chair. Clark stood at a podium at the head of the circle. Morgan and Anderson had been briefed earlier in the car by Wendy on what to expect. Just as the meeting began, Sharon had just arrived and apologized for being late. Another chair was retrieved and placed next to Wendy. At that point Clark asked everyone to be seated. He first turned to John Morgan and asked why he insisted on this meeting and what the urgency was. Morgan told everyone that he wished a time portal to be conjured up so he could go back in time to right a wrong. In other words, he had said that a young boy was saved from drowning in the past but then grew up to be a serial killer. He then produced pictures of the ten dead women. He continued to say that if they had lived, they would have continued to be great contributors to today's society. He urged the coven to allow him to go back to make sure that what happened in the past stayed in the past without any alterations. Before they voted, his last words were, "Remember what happens in the past can affect the present as well as the future. Everything happens for a reason." With that said, he looked at Sharon remorsefully as if to suggest that he was sorry to have to do this. Clark then turned to Sharon and asked for her input. Sharon, with sorrow in her voice, simply said, "I know what must be done must be done. That doesn't make it easy for me to accept. However, since I now know the truth about my brother, I agree that he must be stopped and be stopped before he even gets a chance to hurt anyone else. So, let's just go ahead and get this over with before I change my mind about it." Clark then addressed his coven and said, "Will everyone please stand up and join hands while Mr. Morgan takes his place in the middle of the circle?" After the coven, Wendy, Shelley Anderson, and Sharon stood up and closed ranks to make a circle, John Morgan took his place in the middle. Clark stood at his podium, started swaying back and forth, and chanted the very same chant that was said so many years ago when Sharon was to make the very same trip.

"Goddess of the East, of the West, of the North, of the South, We ask your blessing. We call to you to witness and to guard this circle and all within it. Powers of air and water, of fire and of earth, travel with John now as he travels to the past."

Clark had already given John a slip of paper to chant when his mission was completed. Just as Phillip had instructed Sharon so did Clark instruct John to repeat after him, "I wish to go back; back toward the past; back to when Sharon had returned at 16 on the day her brother had drowned." John repeated the exact words, and Clark, just like Phillip, looked to the heavens and shouted as he closed the incantation with, "Wind, Fire, Water, Earth, I call on you to make this spell magic! So mote it be!"

Just as it happened years ago, the winds swirled and the leaves on the ground began to whirl. A dark blue tunnel loomed above John and surrounded him. He had disappeared along with the blue tunnel. The wind stopped swirling, and the leaves laid flat on the ground just as they were found. The coven and newcomers who were swaying along with Clark had stopped at that point. Now all they could do is wait.

The next thing John knew was that he was at Sharon's old house where she grew up at. He had been instructed that no one could see him except maybe the sixteen-year-old Sharon whom he saw standing just outside. He watched her ascend the stairs into her old room. He followed her. He had been told by Sharon about the notes. He slipped into another room and waited until she had left. John then quietly moved into Sharon's old room, found the notes, and put them into his pocket. He then silently descended the stairs and went to a place where the sixteen-year-old could not see him, not until the young Jason was pronounced dead. When the 13-year-old Sharon failed to save her brother, the sixteen-year-old Sharon was confused as to what had happened. This was when John came out of the shadows and approached her. She looked at him and asked, "Just who in the heck are you?" He said as he handed her his business card, "I am a detective. When you get back to your time period, call me. I will explain everything to you. I know this is confusing, and you want answers. Just do this. That's all I ask." She looked at him tearfully and chanted the words that Phillip gave her. After John had witnessed this, he, too, chanted the same words that Clark had given him, "I wish to go forward in time back to where I said the first rhyme." Just as before, the wind swirled and the leaves whirled. Again, a dark blue tunnel appeared. Then, poof, John was back to his time frame. As he appeared, he gave thumbs up, and with that everyone prepared to go home.

Meanwhile, as the sixteen-year-old Sharon returned to her time, she looked depressed more than ever. She looked at her clothes. They were gothic. This was not to happen. Everything was to turn out better. She just did not understand. She turned to Wen and asked her to take her home. She rushed in the house and went straight to her room without a sound. As she was getting ready for bed, she noticed a business card in one of her pockets. She pulled it out and had looked at it for a few minutes. It was the card that the detective gave to her. He said to call him and that everything would be explained. She decided to call him the next morning.

The next morning, John Morgan and Shelley Anderson were going over some case files when the phone rang. He picked it up and answered, "Morgan here." The voice on the other end meagerly said, "Mr. Morgan? My name is Sharon, and you gave me a card and told me to call you. You said that you would explain everything to me. Is that right?" Morgan just said, "Sharon, I've been expecting your call. Can we meet for a soda or coffee somewhere?" She told him about a coffee house that was not too far from her own house. They both agreed to meet there within an hour. When John arrived, Sharon was already there waiting for him. There were some tables and chairs outside, so that is where they sat. A waiter came and took their orders for two coffees. John looked at her and said, "I'm not sure where to begin, so I'll just start at the beginning." After John had told Sharon the whole story about her brother and what was to happen, Sharon understood. It was at that instance when the guilt finally began to lift. She thanked him and suggested that they both keep in touch. John immediately agreed and told her that if she needed any help or had any more questions to just call him. With that said, they both stood up, and Sharon reached out to give John a big hug. They then said their goodbyes.

Jumping back to John's time frame, he again found himself at his desk going over case files with Shelley. Only this time they were looking at cases that were similar to Jason Foster's case, a child that should have died but didn't then grew up to be a hardened criminal. They both had talked to Clark about the possibility of future time travel. All of a sudden, the phone rang. Morgan picked up the phone and said, "Morgan here." On the other end was a familiar voice that he had become acquainted with through the years. "John? Sharon. Are you free for lunch?" John simply said, "Yeah, Sharon. What's up?" "I just want to say, thank you, and to have lunch with a friend."

Epilogue

Two years had gone by since Morgan had stepped into that time portal when another case file had come across his desk. After looking at it, he walked over to Shelley's desk and plopped it down, "I think we have another Jason, here." That is what they were to name all of the case files that would be similar to what happened to Jason Foster. She thumbed through it, looked up at him, and said, "Well, boss. I do believe that you are right. Only this time we don't have a serial killer but a serial rapist." Even though Morgan had been promoted to Chief of Detectives, he still worked on some cases with Shelley, and now this one would take a special interest to him. "Ok, Anderson, then let's go to work. I'm going to call Clark first and talk to him, then we will start interviewing people to make sure we have another Jason case." Anderson gave him a friendly salute and said, "You ready to go back in time again?" "If it will keep people safe, you betcha I am."

CPSIA information can be obtained
at www.ICGtesting.com
Printed in the USA
BVHW040250110323
660181BV00008B/789